The Predator's Bait

Seth. H . Mumba

Published by Seth. H . Mumba, 2024.

This is a work of fiction. Similarities to real people, places, or events are entirely coincidental.

THE PREDATOR'S BAIT

First edition. July 11, 2024.

Copyright © 2024 Seth. H . Mumba.

ISBN: 979-8227890382

Written by Seth. H . Mumba.

Also by Seth. H . Mumba

The Predator's Bait

Table of Contents

PROLOGUE

The night was dead; the darkness was so thick you could almost feel it. There were no movements of people, only a distant noise from a famous bar broke the spell of the night. A young woman at the furthest corner of Street was just winding up and closing her shop. It had been a long day with little earnings as usual.

"Time to go home and take a nap. I hope the goons are not out yet," the woman thought as she started to walk towards home. On the desolate road cloaked in thick darkness she walked, her thoughts a whirl of concerns and plans. She pondered over the evening ahead, considering what affordable treat she would bring the children. As the weight of the current economic challenge pressed on her mind, she wondered if it would soon start affecting her small business. She shook off her doubts and continued her journey home. Suddenly, she froze; something wasn't right. Her eyes had caught something, a distant movement from the furthest end of the street.

Three figures suddenly emerged from the shadows, their presence instantly changing the atmosphere. Their menacing aura and the way they carried themselves would send shivers down anyone's spine. It was clear to anyone that these were not individuals to be trifled with. The tallest, seemingly the leader gestured towards the direction of the bar with a commanding finger. Without a word, the other two nodded and followed his lead, their steps echoing ominously in the still night.

Inside the bar a symphony of sounds greeted the three men, loud music blared from state-of -the-art speakers, creating a deafening rhythm that resonated through the entire space. Neon lights in hues of different colors flashed around in sync with the beats. The bar was a clear indication of the presence of rich people on the face of the earth. It was adorned with polished chrome accents and plush leather seating, exuding an air of luxury. The atmosphere was a blend of high energy and opulence, a perfect place for the wealthy looking to lose themselves in the night.

The room was full of people; they had to shove people aside to move. They stood at the center of the room, and for a moment they thought they were in the wrong place. Puppet was the first to notice them. Seated at the corner of the room, it was easy for him to see everything, yet it took the three men a few moments to spot him. They headed towards the lone table and sat. No one spoke for some time, and the men started to get nervous. Puppet was the one who broke the silence.

"You're late," puppet said, his voice cutting through the tension like a blade. The boys exchanged uneasy glances, unsure of their next move, prompting puppet to press further.

"So, tell me, what the hell went wrong with your assignment?"

"We couldn't get what you asked for, Don, their leader started to explain

"And why is that?" Puppet demanded, his tone cold and unyielding.

"It was complicated. The information that we were given was barely accurate, there was hardly anything significant that we could do. We couldn't access everything we needed, and the risk escalated, so we decided to abort, "Don finished, his voice filled with frustration.

Puppet's face showed no emotions at all, he slowly reached to his table and refilled his glass.

"Did you cover your tracks well? "Puppet asked, his voice still cold.

"Yes, everything is secure. No one should suspect a thing, "Don assured him.

"Okay, you may leave now, "Puppet dismissed them with a wave of his hand.

The three men exchanged shocked glances; their frustration written all over their faces.

"What about our pay cheque?" Don erupted, his patience wearing thin, he was already breathing with difficulty. Puppet, still with his cold look reached out again and refilled his glass then took a long sip, he laid back and took his time enjoying the sting of his expensive scotch.

"Pay for what? You dint deliver what was asked of you," Puppet replied calmly, emptying his glass in one smooth motion.

"Do you have any idea how much time and money I've invested in this damn assignment? "Don exploded.

Ï couldn't care less about your expenses. If you want compensation, find Roberto and negotiate with him yourself," Puppet retorted, unfazed by Don's rising anger.

"This is utter bullshit! Do you know who I am? Do you know what I could do to Roberto? Don threatened.

"Nah, I don't know; why don't you enlighten me?" Puppet responded with a mocking grin.

Don was on the brink of losing his composure. He couldn't believe the audacity of Puppet's indifference.

"Well fine. You'll regret this. You'll remember me when I expose all your murky activities to the media, that's a promise, "Don spat out bitterly, turning to leave with his gang.

Puppet watched them leave the table and head toward the exit, calmly, he took his bottle of scotch and drained the last bit into his glass and with one gulp, he drained it. He then stood up and followed the three men into the darkness.

Don's enraged complaints echoed through the alleyways. They were so lost in their problems that they hardly noticed the changes in their environment. Suddenly, one of the young man's keen ears caught a faint sound-the unmistakable click of a gun being cocked. They all turned sharply to see a dark figure advancing towards them, gun in hand. Fear gripped them as they realized the danger.

Without hesitation, they scattered, running for their lives. But it was already too late. Three sharp cracks shattered the night air, followed by agonized cries. The three bodies fell to the ground, wailing and cursing in pain, then they stopped, never to move again.

Puppet stood still for a moment, his expression unreadable, calmly he turned away from the scene. The night was silent again, Puppet disappeared into the shadows, leaving behind the chilling aftermath of betrayal.

ONE

12th May, Bangkok, Thailand.

It was on an evening; the dim glow of the street lights illuminated the streets. A sleek, black sedan was inconspicuously parked on a narrow side street. The car's tinted windows cloaked the identities of the three figures inside, their bodies calmly relaxed as they waited for their target.

Jack, Zack and Lacy had once been elite operatives in an organized intelligence force, a trio famed for their efficiency and precision. Their last mission, in Tomsk, however, had not ended as expected, leading to their expulsion from the unit two years prior. Now, disillusioned and hardened, they had turned to a life in the shadows, leveraging their formidable skills for monetary gains.

Jack, the self-proclaimed leader of the trio, sat in the driver's seat, his fingers tapping rhythmically on the steering wheel, a habit that the rest hated but there was nothing they could do. His piercing brown eyes scanned the street through the rear-view mirror, every passing figure subjected to thorough scrutiny. He had a rugged handsomeness about him, with a chiseled jawline and a permanent smirk on his face that gave him an air of dangerous charm.

In the back seat, Zack was busy trying to solve a word puzzle. The former tech specialist of the group, brains of the operation, able to analyse and provide tactical instructions to his team. His years in the forces had granted him the technical skills to hack into the most secure systems and disable alarms with no sweat. His wiry frame and sharp features were often hidden behind a pair of round glasses which he adjusted constantly.

Lacy, sitting in the back seat, was the heart of the team, though her exterior betrayed none of the warmth within. Her short-cropped hair and athletic body made her look every bit of a soldier that she once was. Her eyes, a deep expressive blue, were focused on the tablet on her lap, where she monitored feeds from nearby cameras that Zack had hacked earlier.

"Who cares about the means to make money? Life is short, and then we die. I'm not going to sit around waiting for manna from heaven. Whether you guys are in or not, I'm taking this deal. After all, I'm not being paid to be a patriot," Lacy declared with a wry smile, trying to convince Zack and Jack to accept an offer from an unknown source to raid a group of high school girls.

Zack raised an eyebrow, "So, we just drop everything and trust some anonymous source? This sounds like a disaster waiting to happen."

Jack chuckled, "You always were the cautious one, Zack. But maybe Lacy has a point. We could use the money."

With a reluctant sigh and a shared glance, they agreed to the plan. Days later, they found themselves in Thailand, lying in wait, hearts pounding with a mix of anticipation and dread.

"Hey, Lacy, are you absolutely sure we're in the right place? I don't see any movement at all. Maybe you misread the letter, or we got the date wrong," Zack whispered, his voice tinged with unease.

"Just because you're clueless doesn't mean everyone is. Of course, this is the right place. Give it a few minutes, and we'll be rolling in riches," Lacy snapped back, trying to mask her own nervousness with confidence.

Hours crawled by like molasses, and the tension grew thicker. Zack's patience was wearing thin, "This is taking forever. What if we—"

"Shush! Look," Lacy interrupted, her eyes narrowing.

From the far end of the alley, the group of high school girls appeared, their laughter echoing through the narrow space. They were lost in their conversation, oblivious to the danger lurking in the shadows.

"Show time," Lacy muttered, her heart racing.

With a precision that would make a surgeon jealous, they struck. The raid was swift and silent, leaving the girls stunned and speechless. Within moments, the car was speeding away, the roar of the engine drowning out any chance of pursuit.

As they sped off, Zack couldn't help but laugh, "Well, Lacy, you were right about one thing. We're definitely not getting paid to be patriots."

Lacy grinned, the adrenaline coursing through her veins, "Welcome to the dark side, boys. We're just getting started."

****

Back at the scene, life went on as usual. Women wandered happily through boutiques, searching for the latest fashions. Men stood on street corners, passionately debating politics, their voices rising and falling in animated discussion. Students, backpacks slung over their shoulders, made their way home from school, chattering about their day.

In the local coffee shop, a young boy sat at a table, his eyes wide with shock. Struggling to comprehend what he had just witnessed. Around him, the barista chatted with a regular, and a couple discussed their weekend plans, completely, oblivious to the extraordinary event that had just happened.

✳✳✳✳

As much as she loved her phone, she truly despised the ring tone, especially when it rudely yanked her from sleep like today.

"Hey girl!"

"HI. "Came the bored, sleepy voice of Foxy.

What's up?_ Yeah, I can't wait. _ What are you going to wear? _ Oh gosh! Larry's going to meet her crush," came the excited voice from the other end of the line, brimming with enthusiasm, not waiting for Foxy to give her opinion.

"Yeah, great day. I wish I could come, but it seems my dad had already made plans for me," Foxy replied, her voice quivering with the unmistakable edge of impending tears.

"Oh, come on! Don't tell me your dad made you babysit that thing you call a brother."

"Okay, I won't tell you my dad made me babysit my brother the whole day," Foxy responded, attempting a weak smile through the phone.

"Oh, I'm sorry, Foxy. I wish I could help, but the best I can do is keep you in the loop."

"Okay, thanks. I hope you guys enjoy it. Bye for now, let me answer my call of duty... yeah... you too... bye," and with that, she hung up, a heavy sigh escaping her lips.

All this she remembered vividly as she now sat in their living room, surrounded by the grief-stricken faces of the parents of the missing girls. One couldn't help but feel the weight of their sorrow. Detective Marcus, who had taken charge of the investigation, had bombarded her with all manner of strange questions, yet she, like them, had no clue where her friends Beau, Fein, and Bevy, had vanished to. They had disappeared like the wind, without a single trace.

The boys who had been with them had returned home safely, but they, too, were clueless about the girls' whereabouts.

"Maybe they're just running late," Foxy tried to convince herself. "Maybe they went shopping or got lost or held up somewhere... maybe." She hoped desperately, but deep down, she knew she was fooling herself. Her friends had never stayed out this late; something was horribly wrong.

One by one, the parents began to leave, their fragile hope shattered into pieces. Foxy felt a deep pang of sympathy for them; she wished she could do something to help, but at the same time, she couldn't help but feel a surge of relief. If it hadn't been for her brother, whatever had happened to her friends might have befallen her.

After everyone had left, she decided to take a rest, clinging to the faint hope that tomorrow's breakfast would bring good news and laughter, and that her friends would return home safely. As she lay down, her mind was a battlefield of conflicting thoughts. What could have gone wrong? An accident seemed unlikely; they always preferred to walk, sticking to their usual route from school, past the coffee shops where men wasted their time, and then to their houses. No matter how hard she tried, she couldn't find an answer.

Sleep finally claimed her, but not before her last thought lingered: "Where could they be?"

Foxy's dreams were restless, filled with shadowy figures and unanswered questions. The faces of her friends flashed before her, their expressions a mix of fear and confusion. She reached out for them, but they always slipped through her fingers, like trying to grasp smoke.

Morning came too soon, and for the first time in her life, she wished her phone would just ring.

TWO

It was a dazzlingly bright day, the kind where the sun's golden rays seemed to dance on every surface, illuminating the world with an almost surreal clarity. The sky was a brilliant, unblemished blue, stretching endlessly overhead, while the wind was eerily calm, as if it too were pondering the strange turn of events. Even the trees stood still, their leaves barely rustling, as if nature itself was holding its breath. Amid this serene backdrop, Drago found it increasingly difficult to wrap his head around what Derick was trying to tell him.

"You mean they're no more? They're gone?" Drago's voice trembled, the words barely a whisper, more a plea than a question.

"I just said they're missing. That's what Foxy told me, so don't jump to conclusions yet," Derick replied, his tone a mix of frustration and worry.

Out of the estate, Gavin and Ben appeared, their faces mirroring the shock and disbelief that Drago felt. They looked like they'd just woken from a nightmare, trying to reconcile the sunny day with the dark news they were hearing.

"But... they... I was..." Gavin stammered, unable to form a complete sentence. He sat down on a nearby stone, he felt as if his energy was being sucked out of his body.

"And where's Brasco? He's supposed to be here. Does he know what's going on?" Gavin asked no one in particular. As if on cue, the familiar hoarse voice of Brasco cut through the tension.

"Yo! My friends, what's up?" Brasco's usual swagger was evident, but he stopped abruptly when he saw the somber faces. "Hey! What's up with the stupid looks? Did you guys see a ghost?

No one talked, they all looked at him like he was the most stupid person they had ever seen.

Okay, if you're down, I can tell you a funny story I heard this morning. You see, there's this dude from our neighborhood..."

"We don't care about your neighborhood!" Derick snapped; his patience worn thin. "We're here for serious issues. The girls are missing!"

For a moment, Brasco stood there, processing the words. "What girls?" he asked, just as the gravity of the situation hit him. He fell silent, his mind racing. This was too much to be a mere coincidence.

The five boys sat down on the estate steps, the vibrant day around them contrasting sharply with the dark cloud of worry hanging over them. They wracked their brains, trying to figure out where their friends might have gone. Nearly two hours passed with no breakthrough until Brasco finally spoke up.

"Guys, I have a weird story."

"Really, dude? Is this the time for that?" Derick shot back, his voice rising.

"Just give him a chance," Gavin interjected, sarcasm dripping from his words. "Maybe he can prove he's not as foolish as we think. Go on, Brasco."

"Just be quiet, will you?" Brasco replied, clearly irritated. "This is a true story that happened today. So, some guy was at Manherms Coffee Shop yesterday..."

"Wait! You mean the same coffee shop we all know?" Gavin interrupted.

"I don't think there's another shop with that name, so will you please shut up and let me talk?" Brasco retorted; frustration evident in his voice.

"So, as I was saying, this guy went to the coffee shop yesterday. When he came back home, his mother noticed he looked kind of confused. When she tried to inquire, he told her a story that, to me, can't be a dream, as his parents put it." Brasco took a deep breath, seeing he had his friends' undivided attention.

"This guy said that while he was busy stuffing himself, some four girls passed by the window next to him. Then there was this black car where two men ambushed them, threw them in the car, and drove off." Brasco's face was grave as he finished.

"Okay! Hold up. Don't you think something like that would be all over the news by now?" Drago asked, his brow furrowed with doubt.

"Yeah, something like that can't be missed," Gavin backed him up, nodding in agreement. "It would be plastered across every news outlet and social media feed. Everyone would be talking about it. There would be alerts, bulletins, and people freaking out. It's strange that we haven't heard a peep about it."

"But how come no one else saw that?" Derick asked, disbelief coloring his voice.

"That baffles me too. I think that's why the boy isn't believed. But think about it. Everything makes sense: the girls being kidnapped just a few miles from where we left them, then this black car thing. I saw it for around six days. It was always there, like some lost spaceship. This isn't a coincidence, guys. Our friends have been kidnapped." By now, everyone's face was pale with horror and realization. There was no doubt in their minds that their friends had been taken.

"We need to tell Foxy and also go to this boy to figure out how we're going to help them. I really hope we're not too late," Drago suggested, urgency in his voice.

They all nodded in agreement and set off toward Freeman's house, their only witness. The sunny day now felt oppressive, the weight of their mission pressing down on them.

"By the way, Brasco, one more question," Ben broke the silence as they walked. "Do you mean to tell us you knew all this and just sat there for two hours like some dude frozen like Sub-Zero?"

Brasco just looked at his friends for a moment, then shrugged. "Yes," he replied, with a half-smile that tried and failed to mask his worry. The gravity of their task ahead loomed large, but at least they had a lead, however small, to follow.

****

"Dinner will be ready in twenty minutes, sir," the maidservant announced quietly. Roberto, however, remained oblivious to her presence, his thoughts consumed by his one true passion: money. He stared blankly out the window, the golden hues of the setting sun casting an ethereal glow over his opulent study. Across from him, Puppet sat patiently, his loyalty to Roberto unshakeable. Once a street urchin, Puppet now thrived under Roberto's protection, his devotion as solid as it could be. He needed no army of henchmen like Roberto's rivals; Puppet was more than capable of handling any task.

As Puppet waited, memories of the past washed over him. He remembered the plump, imposing figure of Roberto, the man who had given him a new lease on life. Puppet recalled his own skeletal frame from those days, a stark contrast to the robust man he had become. Time had flown by, bringing with it a flood of changes.

"Boss, what's the plan? We've got sixteen girls now, and if we don't act fast, our luck might run out," Puppet broke the silence, his voice edged with urgency.

Roberto snapped out of his reverie, his eyes sharp and calculating. "I know. Get ready. In seven days, you'll handle the transactions. It'll buy us some time to strategize our next move," he instructed, his voice cool and commanding.

"Understood, sir. Puppet's response was followed by a brief moment of silence.

But there's something else," Puppet hesitated, seeking Roberto's permission to continue.

"Go on," Roberto encouraged, a hint of impatience creeping into his tone.

"Back on the streets, I survived on my instincts. They never let me down. And right now, those instincts are screaming that something's off about this one. Maybe we should pass on it," Puppet confessed, his unease palpable.

Roberto's expression darkened, his eyes narrowing. "Puppet, you will follow my orders. In seven days, make the transactions. No questions, no doubts. Do you understand?" he growled, his voice barely containing his fury.

"Yes, sir," Puppet replied, standing abruptly, then turned and left the room, the heavy door closing behind him with a soft thud.

As Puppet walked down the dimly lit corridor, his mind raced. The mansion's grandeur did little to ease his growing anxiety. His instincts had kept him alive on the streets, and now, they were screaming at him louder than ever. He couldn't shake the feeling that this time, they were diving headfirst into something horrible

Roberto, left alone in his study, returned to his thoughts. He trusted Puppet's instincts but couldn't afford to show weakness or *hesitation. The world they operated in was unforgiving, and any sign of doubt could be their downfall. He stared out the window, the sun now a sliver on the horizon, casting long shadows across the room. The calm before the storm, he thought. And he intended to weather it, no matter the cost.*

Detective Marcus's mind was racing, a whirlwind of thoughts and theories threatening to overwhelm him. Events were unfolding at a breakneck pace, and he felt the weight of urgency pressing down on him. The tall, athletic agent with blonde hair and a deep voice had been summoned while he was shopping with his daughter, Sheila. It was supposed to be a day off, a rare moment of a normal life, but duty called and he answered without hesitation.

"We need to open our minds. Anything you remember will be of great help, "Marcus repeated, his voice edged with desperation. This was the tenth time he'd said it since arriving.

"Come on, Dad! They've told you a hundred times what they know," Sheila complained.

"Yeah, I know, but you guys don't see the real picture. This isn't just what you think it is, "Marcus insisted.

"Do you mind explaining yourself?" Gavin asked, his curiosity palpable.

"Look, there's this cartel that has been wreaking havoc in this city for some time. Unfortunately, no one knows anything about them; they really know how to cover their tracks. Your friends are not the first ones to go missing. They've just added their tally to

sixteen. I'm afraid if we don't act quickly, we might run out of luck, "Marcus explained, his voice low and urgent. The teenagers looked back at him, their faces a mix of fear and determination.

Freeman, a young man with woolen hair and an air of quiet intensity, muttered to no one in particular, "I wish it was as easy as you put it." His face was almost expressionless, making it hard to tell if he was serious or joking.

"Why would you say that?" Ben asked, his tone harsh and skeptical.

"The raid was quick. Within seconds, they had taken off. Whoever is doing this really knows their job. But I believe if we work together, we can make it," Freeman explained, his voice steady. There was a collective murmur of agreement as everyone seemed to rally around his confidence.

As they discussed their plan, the room buzzed with tension. The bait was set, and each person knew their role. There was no room for error. The fate of the missing girls depended on their success. Just as they were about to depart, Detective Marcus called out, "By the way, Freeman, one thing doesn't add up. When you saw the kidnapping, why didn't you do something?"

The room fell silent, all eyes on Freeman. He met Marcus's gaze steadily, but said nothing for a few moments. The pause stretched, thick with anticipation and unspoken fears.

Finally, Freeman broke the silence, his voice quiet but clear. "I was too stunned to believe what I had seen had really happened. It was like a nightmare unfolding before my eyes. By the time I snapped out of it, they were gone."

Marcus's mind churned with this new information. "And you're sure it was them?" he pressed.

Freeman nodded. "Positive. I saw their faces. I'd recognize them anywhere."

A chill ran down Marcus's spine. The cartel was not only efficient but also brazen. They had snatched sixteen girls without leaving a trace, operating with a precision that was almost military. The clock was ticking, and every second brought them closer to losing the girls forever.

As they moved out, Marcus couldn't shake the feeling that something was wrong. The streets were unusually quiet, the air heavy with a sense of impending doom. He glanced at Sheila; her face set in a mask of determination. He had dragged her into this dangerous game, and he prayed he could keep her safe.

In the dimly lit alleyways and shadowed corners of the city, the team moved with caution. Every sound seemed amplified; every movement scrutinized. And then, just as they were about to leave the dark alley, a figure stepped out of the shadows.

"Welcome, Detective," a friendly voice spoke up. I've been expecting you."

$$\text{\ast\ast\ast\ast}$$

It had taken them almost three hours to get where they were going. The trio chatted confidently, believing that in a few hours' time, they would be receiving their paychecks. The sun was setting, casting a golden hue over the landscape, but the dense forest they were driving through was beginning to cloak itself in shadows.

"Who the hell are you people?" Bevy decided to ask, her curiosity piqued despite the odd circumstances.

"Oh, us? Never mind, this is the first and last time you will ever see us. You'll be taken far away where you won't even remember me, I promise," Jack mocked, a sinister smile playing on his lips.

They arrived at their destination, a huge, old building in the middle of nowhere. The compound fence was made up of broken structures, the remnants of what might have once been a grand estate. The place looked abandoned, as if no one had set foot there for years. But little did they know what awaited them.

They were ushered into a dark, foul-smelling room, sprawling on the cold, damp floor. All of them blinked rapidly, trying to adjust to the dense darkness. After nearly two minutes of disorientation, they decided to sit in the corner of the room, feeling their way along the walls.

beau's scream brought everyone back to the present. "What is it, beau?" Bevy asked, but all beau managed to do was point toward the farthest corner of the room. That's when everyone's blood froze. Their eyes registered several figures amidst the darkness. The figures started to advance toward them, and no matter how hard they tried to move away, they couldn't. They were trapped in the corner.

"Hi! I'm Wicham. Has my father come to take me home?" an unfamiliar voice asked, breaking the eerie silence.

"What do you mean, your father?" Fein asked, puzzled but slightly relieved that these figures posed no immediate danger.

"Oh, it's nothing, never mind," Wicham replied, her voice betraying her disappointment.

"Hey! Wicham, do you mind telling us what's going on?" Bella asked, her voice trembling slightly.

"It's simple. We're all kidnapped. And if God doesn't work a miracle, we will be taken to who knows where and I don't know what will happen next," Wicham explained, her tone somber.

"You mean like slave trade?" Fein asked, concern etched on her face.

"If you look at it that way, then yes," Wicham replied with a sigh.

"Okay, take it slow, Wicham. What's really going on?" Bevy pressed again, her mind racing with fear and confusion.

Wicham looked at the girls before her, feeling a pang of pity. She let out a huge sigh before continuing. "Okay, since we will be taken away and this information will be of no help, I guess I will just tell you to pass the time."

The sixteen girls huddled together, drawing some comfort from each other's presence. Wicham began to recount the story behind their predicament.

"It all started a few months ago," Wicham began, her voice steady but tinged with sadness. "There's this cartel operating in the city, kidnapping girls and selling them into slavery. They're efficient, ruthless, and they leave no traces. They've been targeting girls who are alone or in small groups, making them easy targets."

The girls listened intently, their faces a mix of horror and disbelief.

"But why us?" Bella asked, her voice barely above a whisper.

"It's not personal. They're just after easy targets. We were in the wrong place at the wrong time," Wicham explained. "I've been here for weeks, waiting for them to make their move. I hoped my father would find me, but it seems like that's not going to happen."

"Is there any way out of here?" Bevy asked, desperation creeping into her voice.

"I've tried to find a way out, but this place is like a fortress. They've got guards patrolling the grounds, and the exits are all locked," Wicham said, her voice heavy with resignation.

"But there has to be a way," Fein insisted, her determination unyielding. "We can't just sit here and wait for them to take us."

The girls fell into a contemplative silence, the weight of their situation pressing down on them. The room felt colder, the darkness more oppressive. They could hear the distant sounds of the forest outside, the chirping of crickets, and the rustling of leaves, a stark contrast to the silent tension within the room.

Suddenly, the door creaked open, and a shadowy figure entered. The girls tensed; their breath caught in their throats. The figure moved closer, and the dim light from the hallway illuminated his face. It was Jack.

"Enjoying your stay, ladies?" he sneered, his eyes gleaming with malice. "Don't get too comfortable. You won't be here for long."

The door slammed shut behind him, plunging the room back into darkness. The girls exchanged fearful glances, their hope dwindling. But amidst the fear, a spark of determination ignited. They knew they had to find a way out, no matter the cost.

"We need a plan," Bevy whispered, her voice firm. "We can't let them take us without a fight."

The girls nodded in agreement, their resolve strengthening. They huddled together, whispering their ideas and strategies, determined to outsmart their captors. The night stretched on, filled with whispered plans and silent prayers. They knew the odds were against them, but they also knew they had to try. For their freedom, for their lives.

"Do you know the person in charge of these men, Wicham?" beau asked, his curiosity unabashed.

"Yeah," Wicham replied, a hint of reluctance in his voice. "I know quite a lot about him, actually. Trust me, he's not someone you'd want to meet."

Bevy leaned in; her impatience palpable. "Who is he, then?"

Seeing no way out, Wicham took a deep breath and began to recount the story of the man whose greed had ensnared them all.

****

Roberto. The name alone conjured an image of a man whose very presence could make a room grow cold. He was short and plump, with a stout posture that belied a hidden strength. His silky hair, once a rich brown, now flowed down to his neck in a glittering cascade of silver-Gray, a testament to the years he had endured. A protruding goatee jutted out like a stubborn stump on his round chin, while his thick neck supported a small, round head that seemed almost comically mismatched to his body.

Born in Brazil, Roberto's early years were marred by tragedy and hardship. His mother had died under mysterious circumstances when he was just ten years old, and the loss had driven his father into a bottle, leaving Roberto to fend for himself. His childhood in the streets was a living hell, filled with dangers and bad influences that would shape the man he would become.

Roberto's journey took him to the far corners of the world. He grew up in China, where he learned the art of survival and the value of power. In Russia, he found love and married, but the union was short-lived. After a bitter divorce, he made his way to Germany, where he finally settled. It was here that he truly flourished, though not in any noble sense. Roberto immersed himself in the murky underworld, dealing in drugs and human trafficking. His name became synonymous with fear and corruption.

He loved money with a passion that bordered on obsession. Roberto would stop at nothing to increase his wealth, even if it meant taking extreme measures. There were whispers that he would even consider murdering himself if it meant adding a few more digits to his account. His ruthlessness knew no bounds.

Wicham paused, letting the gravity of his words sink in. "Those goons who brought you here," he continued, his voice dropping to a conspiratorial whisper, "they work for him. In a few days, I don't think we'll still be here."

beau and Bevy exchanged uneasy glances, the weight of Wicham's revelation settling heavily on their shoulders. The air seemed to thicken with suspense, each of them grappling with the realization of the danger they were in. Roberto's reach was long and his influence pervasive. Escape seemed a distant hope, and they could only wonder what fate awaited them under the watchful eye of the man who controlled their captors.

"Just then, the door to the room flung open, and an athletic figure stood framed in the doorway, holding their meals. She didn't say a word; her presence alone commanded attention. Her movements were swift and precise as she crossed the room, opened the dishes, and set them down. The aroma of the food wafted through the air, tantalizing and unexpected. Without so much as a glance, she exited the room, closing the door behind her with a decisive click.

"I didn't expect them to offer such nice food," Fein commented, breaking the silence. The delicious smell of the meal filled the room, momentarily distracting them from their predicament.

"That's because we'll soon be taken off," Wicham said, his tone grim. "We need to look presentable."

Fein and the others exchanged uneasy looks, the reality of their situation settling in once more. The luxurious meal, so out of place in their captivity, was a stark reminder of the unknown fate that awaited them. They knew they had to be ready for whatever lay ahead, their senses heightened by the ever-present tension and the foreboding atmosphere that clung to the room.

****

""What! Imprisoned for life? This can't be happening," Puppet thought, his mind reeling as he stared at the stern face of the judge who had just pronounced his sentence. The words echoed in his ears, their finality settling in like a heavy weight on his chest. Desperately, he looked around the courtroom, scanning the faces in the crowd for any sign of his allies. But there was no one. Roberto was nowhere to be seen. Instead, the cold, piercing eyes of his enemies bore into him, their silent triumph palpable.

And then, the laughter began. It started as a low murmur but quickly grew into a cacophony of wicked, mocking laughter that seemed to fill the entire room. Puppet could feel it resonating in his bones, a sinister force that threatened to consume him. The world around him spun, a dizzying blur of faces and noise. He lost his balance, his vision darkening at the edges, and just as he felt himself slipping into oblivion...

He woke up with a jolt, his body drenched in sweat. The oppressive weight of the dream lifted, replaced by the sudden, disorienting relief of waking. His heart pounded in his chest, the adrenaline still coursing through his veins. It took him a moment to realize that the sound that had pulled him from his nightmare was his ringtone. He fumbled for his phone, his hands trembling, and answered it.

"Hey! Good news for me," came Roberto's cheerful voice, jarringly out of place after the terror of the dream. He didn't bother with greetings. "There's some sort of party organized by a nearby school. It's for some teenagers. I think you know what to do. Get them ready before market day, and remember, the more fish you catch, the richer I become." The line went dead, the beeping signal indicating that Roberto was done talking.

Puppet sat in the darkness; the phone still clutched in his hand. His body felt tight, his muscles coiled with tension. His heart continued to pound, a relentless drumbeat in his chest. Slowly, the reality of Roberto's words sank in, and a cold dread settled over him. His brain started to sing a familiar, haunting tune—a song of warning, a premonition of danger and revenge that loomed on the horizon.

The remnants of the dream clung to him, a spectral reminder of the peril he faced. Puppet knew he had to act, and fast. The line between his nightmares and his waking life was blurring, and he could no longer ignore the signs. The danger was real, and it was coming for him.

****

"Ben's voice cut through the tense silence, "You really think this will work?" He wasn't speaking to anyone in particular, but the weight of his words settled heavily in the room.

Mr. Clock, his face etched with lines of worry and desperation, responded, "We really hope so. This is my only chance to get my daughter back." His voice trembled slightly. Mr. Clock, the father of Wicham, had spent what felt like an eternity hoping for this moment. He had seen a glimmer of hope, like a shooting star streaking across the night sky. For the first time in many days, he dared to dream of seeing his daughter again.

Brasco's voice broke through the momentary silence, a mixture of confusion and frustration. "Guys, I know you will find this normal, but I really don't get it. Why did Roberto go for your daughter when you were the real danger?"

Mr. Clock sighed deeply; the weight of his sorrow almost palpable. "Life is unfair, son. It is so unfair."

The room fell silent again, each person feeling the heavy burden of Mr. Clock's pain. They all felt sorry for him, but there was nothing they could do to ease his suffering.

Nearly four hours had passed since they arrived, and the air was thick with anticipation and dread. The world outside seemed oblivious, people laughing and enjoying their night, while this small group was holding their breath, praying that everything would go according to plan.

Just when hope was starting to wane, the moment they had been waiting for finally arrived. A black car parked nearby, blending into the night like any other vehicle, but to this group, it was anything but ordinary. Three figures sat inside, unmoving, their presence sending a shiver down the spines of those watching.

Everyone took their positions, and Mr. Clock felt a flicker of hope. Yet, the fear that his daughter might not be any more restrained his emotions. They watched as the trio made their move, swift and silent. No one else noticed as they snatched up three girls with chilling efficiency. The car sped away, and for a moment, the world seemed to stand still.

Then, the van they had so carefully positioned roared to life and entered the main road, following the black car into the darkness.

THREE

They all sat on the cold cement floor, each lost in her own world, grappling with the sudden and terrifying changes in their lives. None of them had ever imagined something like this could happen. Dread and anxiety filled their hearts. Every passing second reminded them they were captives, and there was nothing they could do about it.

The rising chorus of complaints brought them back to reality. The shrill cries of "Let me go!" and "Leave me alone!" signaled that their numbers were about to grow.

The door flew open, and three girls were thrown inside, sprawling on the floor. Flora, one of the original captives, was the first to move. She rushed over to console them. When the newcomers finally composed themselves, they began to explain how they ended up in this dark room.

"What was the name of the party?" Fein asked after listening to their story.

"Well... it was a weird name. I think something like the Toasted Dance Party... or... yeah, that was it."

Fein's face lit up with sudden recognition. "A clue, they've sent us a clue!"

"What clue?" Bevy asked, confused.

"Come on, think! What codeword do we use?" Fein shot back.

Realization dawned on Bevy. "Oh! I get it now."

"Can you guys fill us in?" Wicham asked, still puzzled.

"Toasted is our group slogan," Fein explained.

"So?" Wicham was still confused.

"Okay, I get it, but who in their right mind chose that slogan? It's so weird," Wicham said, and they all chuckled, briefly lightening the mood.

Suddenly, the door swung open again, and everyone's blood ran cold. Their hearts stopped for a moment as they saw the dark figure standing at the entrance. Time seemed to freeze. The figure stood there motionless, like someone with no purpose. He then entered the room and walked to the furthest corner. A few seconds later, the room was flooded with light, surprising the girls, who had no idea the room had electricity. As their eyes adjusted to the light, the man took an old stool and sat facing them.

"Hello, ladies," he began. "I am Phashti, but you can call me Puppet. Of course, you already know I am Roberto's right-hand man."

"We don't care who you are or what you do. We want to go home," Bella shot back.

Puppet grinned. "No, I have a better idea. I'll tell you a story."

The girls couldn't believe what they were hearing. "You're crazy," beau said, her voice filled with venom. But they knew there was no point in arguing.

"Where I was born, or who my parents were, I might never know," Puppet began. "When I gained my senses, I was already on the streets. I came to regard it as my home, a refuge from this mad world. But life wasn't easy. I never knew where my next meal was coming from. I grew up in hardship, which shaped my life and made me a survivor."

He paused, looking at the girls. Seeing he had their full attention, he continued. "One day, I had nothing to eat. I was so hungry, I thought I was going to die. In my desperation, I decided to try my luck at a high-end hotel. It was massive, reserved for the wealthy. Just looking at its offerings made me want to cry. But when I finally managed to sneak inside, everyone was shocked by my appearance. I was an itch to the rich. But there was this man who invited me over to his table. He bought me food I had never tasted before. I told him my life story, and he offered to adopt me. This man was Roberto.

I lived with him for quite some time. He taught me the ways of the murky world and the civilized world. But there were things he couldn't teach me, things the streets had taught me: my survival instincts. Roberto liked me because of my intelligence. No cop has ever dreamed of laying hands on me. Catching me would be one of the greatest achievements this city has ever made.

One of my special abilities is my sixth sense, my instincts never lie to me. It like my guardian angel, any signs of danger and my mind bursts with songs of warning.

"Excuse me, Mr. Puppet," Wicham interrupted. "What does this weird song of yours say?"

"Oh, nice. I thought you wouldn't ask. It depends on the situation. For instance, right now, my head is singing a very sorrowful song."

Puppet closed his eyes and began to recite:
"Run, my child, for danger awaits.
Run, my son, run for your precious life.
The shelter above you will soon crumble.
Run, my friend, for revenge and betrayal await."

He finished his song and opened his eyes, looking at the girls with pity. "Hey, Mr. Puppet, why are you telling us this?" beau asked.

Instead of answering, he pulled a gadget from his pocket and handed it to Wicham. "Give this to your father. Tell him the password is 'hostility.'

"You're a psycho." Fein said.

"And why should I trust you?" Wicham asked, her voice full of venom.

"You don't have to, but it's the right thing to do. Have a nice day," Puppet replied. He rose and left, closing the door behind him.

The girls looked at each other, a glimmer of hope appearing at the end of their dark tunnel.

"What's that he gave you?" one of the girls asked.

"I don't know. Let's take a closer look," Wicham said. They all huddled around her. It was a hard drive.

"Does anyone know what this means?" Wicham asked. Everyone nodded, realizing that this might be their chance.

FOUR

Ten minutes past noon, Roberto's phone screen flashed incessantly: seven missed calls and several unread messages. He noted them but chose to ignore the chaos they hinted at. The troublesome people could wait; he had all the time in the world. Right now, he would focus on the most important thing in his life: money.

He settled into his favorite seat, letting the smooth strains of classical music from his expensive sound system wash over him. His peace was momentarily disturbed by the movements of his many workers, who diligently ensured the majestic bungalow remained in perfect order. Soon, even the music failed to hold his interest. He turned it off and began to think about money again.

Only three days remained until the completion of a significant transaction. He now had nineteen girls. "They would bring in a lot of dough," he thought, marveling at the figures. Yet, something gnawed at him—Puppet. He had warned him about running out of luck. Roberto trusted Puppet's instincts. "But even Goliath was once defeated," he mused, pushing the uneasy thought away.

A sharp ring from his phone yanked him back to the present. The same number had been persistently calling. Annoyed, he decided to answer and get it over with.

"What do you want? I don't have time for your silly baby cries," Roberto snapped.

"Sir, we have a problem!" the voice on the other end trembled.

"None of my damn business," Roberto interrupted curtly.

"Sir, just listen to me. We've been tracked down. The toasted party was just a bait. The whole agency is coming after you. Things wouldn't have been worse if you had just picked up my first call."

Roberto's world tilted. The revelation was a punch to the gut. Unbelievable, yet undeniable. He forced himself to stay composed.

"Arrange for me an immediate flight. I'll be there in an hour. Understood?"

"Yes, sir. And what about puppet?" the voice hesitated.

Roberto glanced at his watch and stood up, his mind racing. "He can burn in hell for all eternity."

****

"Helbron, Harvey Street, the abandoned house—that's where they are. Squad one and two will surround the building. I want two drones sent ahead to monitor their movements. Squad GD and G1 are coming with me," Mr. Clock barked, his voice cutting through the tension in the room like a knife. The troops, clad in their tactical gear, nodded in unison.

Clock swiftly moved to the changing chamber, shedding his civilian clothes for the sleek, dark uniform of the M45 Special Forces. The gear was state-of-the-art, designed for both protection and agility. He donned a bulletproof vest, night vision goggles, and an earpiece for communication, feeling the familiar weight settle on his shoulders.

"There's no time for phone calls, soldier! Get back to your work!" Clock shouted at an officer who hesitated with a ringing phone in hand. The officer snapped to attention and resumed his duties. Within minutes, the troops were ready and the convoy had departed, engines roaring as they sped towards their destination.

"We're coming too," Bevy insisted, her tone leaving no room for argument. Mr. Clock wanted to refuse, but he knew they were integral to the plan's success. Reluctantly, he nodded.

The Special Forces were elite for a reason. Trained in the most rigorous conditions, they excelled in stealth and precision. As they approached the abandoned house, they moved with the silent efficiency of predators. Despite the massive, heavy doors and the high-tech electric security system, they infiltrated the compound without alerting the lion-sized guard dogs patrolling the perimeter.

Each squad took their assigned positions, waiting for Clock's signal. The tension was palpable as they waited in the shadows, every sense heightened.

"Everyone, move in and find the girls. I'll look for that doll," Clock commanded, his voice steady through the earpiece. The squads dispersed, each soldier moving with practiced stealth.

From his vantage point by a dusty window, Puppet watched the intruders with a detached curiosity. He had been monitoring their movements, impressed by their coordination and skill. They had made no noise, but the sudden shift in the song of the night had alerted him. He watched as the troops infiltrated the compound, noting their efficiency.

"But none can match what I can do," Puppet thought, a cold smile spreading across his face.

He saw Mr. Clock approaching, his figure illuminated briefly by a shaft of moonlight. Puppet glanced at his watch, then walked over to a makeshift bar in the corner, pouring himself a glass of whiskey. He picked up his phone, the screen confirming his worst fears. There was no need to call Roberto; the man had left him to fend for himself, leaving him to burn in hell for all eternity.

****

One by one, the guards went down. The squad moved through the house with precise, coordinated movements, swiftly cuffing hands and securing the area. Mr. Clock, ever the strategist, instructed the squad to split up and cover more ground. He moved southwards toward the main room, his senses on high alert. As he entered the room, he saw him.

"Don't move!" Mr. Clock ordered, his voice cold and commanding. Puppet, standing calmly, already knew he was there.

"Hello, Mr. Clock. It's an honor to meet you. Come and join me," Puppet said without turning to face him, his voice devoid of emotion.

"Stop playing games with me, fool. I want the girls right now," Clock demanded, his patience wearing thin.

"Oh, don't worry. The girls are doing just fine. You'll see them soon," Puppet replied, his calm demeanor unshaken.

Mr. Clock felt a flush of relief. His daughter was still alive. He motioned to his men, and two soldiers entered the room, handcuffing Puppet and leading him outside.

"You know this is the end of the road, Puppet," Clock said as they walked.

"Yes, and the beginning of a new one," Puppet replied cryptically, his steps steady and unhurried as he was escorted towards the car.

"I hate dealing with smart criminals," Clock muttered to himself, frustration seeping into his voice.

There was joy and laughter when the lost friends reunited. At last, they were free; they could go home. "And who are these two?" Bevy asked, her curiosity piqued.

"Oh, them... This is Sheila, and this is Freeman. They helped us find you," Foxy explained, doing the introductions. Meanwhile, Wicham had already left to look for her father. She had already forgotten how mad she was.

After the long reunification, they got in their van and started their journey home. Puppet was being escorted to prison.

As the convoy disappeared into the distance, a green motorbike approached the now-quiet compound. The rider, clad in black and moving with deliberate caution, scanned her surroundings several times to ensure she wasn't being followed. She was late, and she knew it. She needed to hurry, as everything depended on her actions.

Quickly, she moved to the point she had been instructed to reach. She found the carefully hidden parcel, confirmed its contents, and placed it in her backpack. Without wasting a second, she got back on her bike and rode off northwards, her heart pounding. The hardest part of her mission was just beginning.

✸✸✸✸

After everyone had reunited with their family members, they decided to relax with a cup of coffee at Manherms Coffee Shop. The atmosphere was light, and laughter filled the air. Even Marcus and Clock seemed to have let go of the tension, enjoying the moment as if nothing had happened. But then, Wicham reached into her jacket for her phone and froze.

"Oh! Guys, the hard drive."

"The what?" Brasco, who was clueless about the situation, asked.

"Do you still have it?" Bella inquired, ignoring Brasco's confusion.

"Yeah! It's here. I almost forgot I had it," Wicham replied, pulling out the hard drive.

"Are we missing something?" Detective Marcus asked, sensing the shift in the atmosphere.

"It's a long story, but Puppet gave this to you," Wicham explained.

"Okay! Wait, Puppet gave me a present?" Clock was visibly shocked.

"How the hell am I supposed to know, Dad?" Wicham responded, rolling her eyes.

"I think Puppet knew he was being set up, so he decided to leave a clue, or maybe... I don't know," Freeman suggested, trying to piece things together.

"Makes sense to me. It's possible, considering he's Roberto's right-hand man," Ben commented, nodding.

"That's cool! So, you guys can now find him easily. What do you think, Gavin?" Drago asked, looking hopeful.

"I'm so lost, so lost. I have no idea," Gavin admitted, shaking his head.

"But it doesn't add up to me. How did Roberto know we were coming for him?" Derrick asked, voicing what everyone else was thinking.

"And Puppet didn't even resist his arrest," Clock realized aloud.

"And he didn't even look worried," Marcus added.

They all sank into their own thoughts, trying to connect the loose ends of the story. The café's waiters and workers noticed their intense focus and wisely chose to keep their distance.

"Guys, I think I've got something," Brasco suddenly broke the silence.

"What is it?" everyone asked, turning their attention to him.

"Take a look at this. Puppet has left you clues. It's not like he's decided to remain silent during interrogation," Brasco explained, pausing to gauge their reactions. Seeing no sign of understanding, he continued, "C'mon, no one willingly goes to prison unless he knows he's not going to stay there."

Realization dawned on everyone. Clock and Marcus exchanged worried glances, uncertain of what to do next. Just then, Clock's phone rang. The group stood up; tension palpable in the air. Clock sighed heavily; they didn't need to answer the call to know that something had gone terribly wrong.

Four armed guards flanked Puppet as he alighted from the car, his chains clinking with every step. He walked steadily towards the massive gates of the prison, his face calm and inscrutable.

"The world is a funny place, isn't it?" Puppet mused aloud, directing his question to one of the guards.

"Shut your trap!" the guard barked, his grip tightening on his weapon.

Puppet ignored the warning and continued, his voice smooth and unperturbed. "I mean, what's the point of living a meaningless life, a life full of malice and greed? It's such a pity that man, with all his intelligence, could do such things. I just wish man would coexist, live in harmony, and help those who are suffering."

"I'm the one who's supposed to be telling you this," the guard retorted, a hint of irony in his tone.

"Yeah, you're right. That's why I'm going to make things right," Puppet said, a cryptic smile playing on his lips.

"I don't think there's much you can do inside prison," the guard replied, dismissively.

"Yeah, I know that," Puppet murmured more to himself. "I am aware of that."

Suddenly, the distant roar of a motorbike echoed through the air. To anyone else, it might have been just another passing bike. The guards initially thought nothing of it, but their complacency was shattered when the rider unleashed a barrage of tear gas canisters.

The guards were instantly enveloped in a choking cloud, their eyes burning and lungs seizing as they struggled to breathe. They coughed and wheezed, their grips faltering on their weapons. In the chaos, Puppet moved with ease, slipping out of his restraints with a deftness that suggested long preparation.

By the time the smoke began to clear, the guards were still disoriented, their senses reeling from the attack. Puppet had vanished, leaving only the faint scent of gas and the echo of the motorbike's engine in his wake.

Realization dawned on the guards as they stumbled back to their feet, their eyes darting around in a futile attempt to locate their escaped prisoner. Puppet had planned his escape with precision, and now he was free, his plan set in motion.

As Puppet sped away on the motorbike, he glanced back at the prison, a small smile of satisfaction curling on his lips. He had outwitted his captors once again, and now, the real game was about to begin.

FIVE

Puppet sat in his hideout, the familiar strains of classical music filling the room. His mind, however, was miles away. It had been only six hours since he had slipped through the fingers of the police. He didn't have to run far; he knew they could never catch him. He imagined them now, crowding airports and ports, trying in vain to track him down. They might as well give up and go home.

"Well? What's your next move?" Daisy asked, emerging from the shower, her eyes still red from the tear gas.

"Roberto," Puppet replied, his voice low and steady.

"Who is your what?" Daisy looked puzzled, drying her hair with a towel.

"Roberto. He's my next move," Puppet repeated, his eyes darkening with determination.

"C'mon, you can't be serious. The cops have your face plastered everywhere. It's too risky," Daisy cautioned, her concern evident.

"You know those cops are a bunch of useless fellows. They won't get me," Puppet retorted, a hint of a smile playing on his lips.

Daisy sighed, recognizing the futility of arguing. She knew Puppet too well; once he set his mind on something, there was no turning back.

"He used me. I really can't believe that jerk dumped me after all I've done for him," Puppet fumed, his fists clenching.

"Are you really that surprised?" Daisy asked, her voice softening.

"Not really, but I will make him feel sorry. I will haunt him like a ghost until he begs for mercy," Puppet vowed, his eyes glinting with cold resolve.

"And how are you planning to do that?" Daisy inquired, genuinely curious.

Puppet sat back, lost in thought. After a few moments, he gave a strange, almost eerie smile. "Honestly... I don't know."

Daisy raised an eyebrow. "You're going after him without a plan?"

"Oh, I'll come up with one. I always do," Puppet said confidently. "Roberto thinks he's untouchable, but he has no idea what's coming for him. I know every move he'll make, every hideout he'll run to. I know his weaknesses."

Daisy looked at him, a mix of admiration and fear in her eyes. "Just be careful. Revenge can cloud your judgment."

Puppet nodded, though his mind was already racing ahead, plotting his next steps. He imagined Roberto's face when he realized Puppet was still out there, still a threat. The thought fueled his determination.

As the night wore on, Puppet and Daisy discussed potential strategies. Daisy, despite her initial reservations, couldn't help but get drawn into Puppet's plans. They talked about possible allies, ways to gather intelligence, and the best approach to take Roberto down.

Puppet's mind was a maze of ideas, each more ruthless than the last. He knew Roberto would be expecting a direct confrontation, so he needed to be unpredictable. He needed to strike when and where Roberto least expected it.

As dawn approached, Puppet's plan began to take shape. He would start by gathering information, finding out who Roberto was dealing with, and what his current operations were. Puppet had contacts, people who owed him favors, and he would call them in.

He would slowly dismantle Roberto's empire, piece by piece, until there was nothing left.

And then, when Roberto was at his most vulnerable, Puppet would make his move.

"Are you sure about this?" Daisy asked one last time, her voice filled with concern.

"Surer than I've ever been about anything," Puppet replied, his eyes steely with resolve.

With that, Puppet rose from his chair, the first light of dawn casting a pale glow over his face. The game had begun, and Puppet was ready to play.

"Roberto's rage filled the room like a furnace, his voice booming with fury. "You want to tell me all this is caused by a bunch of useless teenagers and that Puppet is not arrested?" he shouted; his face red with anger.

"Yes, sir," his subordinate replied, his voice steady but nervous.

"This is not good," Roberto muttered, pacing back and forth. "What about puppet? Do you know his whereabouts? We can still persuade him."

"No, sir. You also know he can't be traced," the man replied, shaking his head.

"Find those kids. They must pay for their sins. I won't allow them to continue interfering with my affairs," Roberto ordered, his voice icy with determination.

"Yes, sir," the man replied, quickly leaving to carry out the orders.

Back home, life had seemingly returned to normal. The teenagers had resumed their normal lives, but a hidden feeling of restlessness lingered beneath their composed exteriors. Each of them felt the weight of unfinished business pressing on their minds. They all wanted one thing: to find Roberto and make him pay.

Despite their burning desire for revenge, they understood the importance of patience. They knew that time would reveal the right moment. For now, they had to be content with what they had accomplished, though the longing for justice simmered just beneath the surface.

Each day, as they attended classes and participated in school activities, their thoughts were never far from the events that had transpired. During lunch breaks and after-school meet ups, they discussed possible plans, gathering intelligence and waiting for the perfect opportunity.

They knew that Roberto wouldn't rest until he found them. The teenagers had become adept at blending in, maintaining a façade of normalcy while always staying vigilant. They had learned to be cautious, to look over their shoulders, and to communicate in code.

In the quiet moments before sleep, each of them thought about what lay ahead. They knew that patience and careful planning would be their greatest allies. They had to be meticulous, leaving no stone unturned, no detail overlooked.

The days turned into weeks, and the weeks into months. They continued to gather information, slowly piecing together the puzzle of Roberto's operations. Each new discovery brought them one step *closer to their goal. They knew the time would come when they would face Roberto again, and when that moment arrived, they would be ready.*

For now, they waited, biding their time, knowing that every passing day brought them closer to justice.

"Hello, everyone. This is Agent Jesse," Clock announced, drawing the attention of the unit. All eyes turned towards the new recruit, a young man with an athletic build and a striking presence. His dark complexion and silky hair added to his mysterious aura as he settled into his desk.

"Hey there!" The team greeted in unison, welcoming Jesse with friendly nods and smiles before returning to their tasks.

"Hi, I'm Charlie," Jesse's neighbor introduced himself. "It's nice to meet you."

"Same here. What's your unit?" Jesse asked, eager to settle into his new role.

"I think they called it G1 or something," Charlie replied with a grin. "Oh, great! So, we're in the same unit."

"Great, at least I won't be lost around here," Jesse chuckled, feeling more at ease already.

"You know, you remind me of my little brother. His name is also Jesse," Charlie remarked, trying to make conversation.

"Oh, that's great. I hope he's a nice fellow," Jesse replied, genuinely interested.

"Yeah, of course, he's a nice chap... What about you? Do you have any brothers?" Charlie continued, unaware of the sensitive topic he was about to touch upon.

"I used to have a brother," Jesse replied quietly, his expression turning somber.

"Oh... I'm so sorry, I shouldn't have asked," Charlie apologized, realizing his misstep.

"Don't be. It's part of life. The best I can do for him is to make sure his killer is brought to justice," Jesse said, his voice firm with determination.

"Do you have any clue who killed your brother?" Charlie asked, his curiosity piqued.

"Yeah," Jesse replied, his gaze piercing. *"The same man who escaped from the agency a few weeks ago."*

"Wait, are you talking about puppet?" Charlie exclaimed, shocked by the revelation.

"My investigation has led me to believe that. I am confident he is my brother's killer," Jesse stated with conviction, his jaw clenched.

"I can't believe this... Every time we think we've seen the last of him, the invincible Puppet strikes again," Charlie murmured, shaken by the news.

"Wow! I didn't know he was called that," Jesse remarked, his mind racing with thoughts.

"Well, we named him that due to his ability to disappear into thin air," Charlie explained, a touch of bitterness in his voice.

"Yeah, I've heard of his ability too. But I wonder how those kids managed to trace him," Jesse pondered aloud.

"Yeah, that also baffles me. But I think they're a bunch of smart kids," Charlie acknowledged, impressed despite himself.

"Of course, they're smart. And I bet they could be very useful," Jesse said, a grin spreading across his face.

"What do you mean?" Charlie asked, curious about Jesse's intentions.

"I mean, if they could find him once, they can do it again. If I can persuade them, I think they will be of great help," Jesse explained, his eyes bright with determination.

"I can also help... if you don't mind," Charlie offered, eager to contribute.

"Thanks, dude. Of course, I need your help. I can't wait to bring that bastard to justice," Jesse replied, his voice filled with resolve.

"So, does that mean the hunt has begun?" Charlie inquired, sensing the seriousness of their conversation.

"Yes, the hunt has begun. And the prey better watch his back," Jesse declared, his focus now squarely on the mission ahead.

As they exchanged nods of understanding, the determination in Jesse's eyes mirrored the unwavering resolve of the entire team. They were ready to embark on a new phase in their fight against Puppet, driven by justice and a shared commitment to righting the wrongs of the past.

~~The end~~

Check out on the next page for a peak at the next story

PROLOGUE

Robi was running as fast as he could. He was determined to put much distance as possible between him and his pursuers, but as hard as he tried, they always seemed to catch up with him. Through the dense forest, Robi tried to remember what he had always learned throughout his life. Keep to the shadows, light as a feather, blind spots and hiding in plain sight. All this he put into practice but it was made worthless by the fact that his pursuers were the infamous Shirma's. Flashes of the previous events ran through his mind, he played everything that had happened from the very beginning to the point where he was running for his dear life.

It took him a while to realize that he had not eaten for the past two nights, his body had only survived on water that was in abundant at the forest, he was super exhausted, but his pursuers who seemed to have an endless supply of energy did not seem willing to give him a chance to regain his energy.

On the third night, the Shirma's were nearly catching up, and so it was a relief when the forest suddenly engulfed Robi in a thick cloud of darkness and he saw this as an opportunity to have a rest, at a place like this, even the mighty Shirma's would be busy watching their backs.

"Hey! Robi, you don't have to do this, you don't have to be the hero today, we can talk this through like men and everyone gets to go home to their families." The hoarse voice of Gongbao, the captain of the Shirma's echoed through the dark forest.

"Or maybe you could just go home and stop wasting your time old man." Robi replied in a mocking tone.

Gong bao was now on the verge of erupting, his face was now red with hot furry, in no time the entire region will know that the mighty Shirma's were unable to get one useless peasant. His ego could not handle this kind of scandal, right now his entire career, not to mention his big head depended on the outcome of this.

"c'mon Robi, you don't have to be stubborn like this, think about your family, think about the wealth you could get if you only chose to cooperate with us, try to think what would happen to your precious Sophia if you choose to continue down this path."

The mention of his wife nearly got to Robi, it took all his self-control to prevent him from running to the talking bastard and chock him to death with his own bare hands. Images of his lovely Sophia flashed through his mind, the lovely voice and his wonderful smile was all he needed to get his strength back. Now with renewed determination, he was willing to run to the end of the world just to keep everyone safe. "Are you always this boring?" robi shot back at gangbao who was still talking. "you guys should just give up; I'm not giving you anything."

At this point Gongbao had had enough of this mockery, he was willing to torch down the whole forest just to get him but just like Robi, his years of training taught him otherwise.

"So, this is how it's going to be? Huh! You're just going to throw away your whole life for something that's not even worth fighting for. You see, that's the problem with peasants like you, you never see the bigger picture, you're always too shallow minded to reason with logic. People like you don't matter Robi, you are just some things that happen to occupy the space that people like us who matter need. Now I'm going to give you another chance to hand over the scroll, otherwise you'll not like what I do to you when I finally get you."

"Wow, you really talk a lot, just please go home and stop wasting our time here Gongbao." Robi continued with his mockery

Gongbao was now out of patience, he scanned the environment carefully, in this dense darkness like this, he had to use his brains if he was to capture his fugitive. He then came up with a plan, he signaled his right-hand man and he got ready to execute his orders. "Hey Robi, where are you?"

"Please don't tell me you are that stupid." Robi answered. And that was all the signal Gongbao needed. An arrow was let loose in the air, like hot knife on butter it sliced through the air and it landed perfectly on Robi's shoulder.

Its pain came to him as a surprise, for a second, he was struck numb, but his survival skills kicked in almost immediately, he stood up and just like before, the chase continued. The arrow had somehow interfered with his sense of judgement, his senses were lowered and he didn't seem to notice his environment. His left foot was the first to trip, then his whole body followed down the cliff.

✱✱✱✱

It had just stopped raining, the slow drip of the water from the roof into the metal bucket at the center of the room seemed to have entranced the young woman at the house. She had just finished making her meal, but for some reason, she just couldn't bring herself to eat it. Slowly she started to ponder on the current things that had being happening, since the new young king had taken control over the kingdom, things had just gotten out of hand. Taxes had been raised and poverty had suddenly become a normal thing, peasants like her who only depended on farming for their upkeep were now supposed to provide two fifths of their produce to the army for free as a sign of their loyalty, those who had refused had found themselves facing crime charges that were never had of since the foundation of their kingdom. The people of the kingdom had already started missing their previous king who was the exact contrast of his son, he had died of a mysterious disease, at least that is what the officials said but many speculated that he was probably poisoned by his evil son who had only wanted ultimate power over the kingdom.

The woman then stood up to empty the bucket which had already filled to the brim, she came back and since she still had no appetite for her food she continued with her thoughts. She remembered how after a long period of suffering, one man from the previous king's council started a fierce rebellion against the throne, even though it took him only a few weeks to find himself in prison, he had already started a fire that was never to be quenched. And for a moment, the kingdom had hope again that thing would change for the better.

The woman finally decided that he no longer needed her meal and thought it wise that she retires to bed early. Just as she was about to go, a wild knocking was heard at her door. At a desolate village like hers, chances that it was a thief were very slim. A few moments later another wild knock came and the woman was convinced that this was urgent as so she opened the door and a young man came rushing in looking confused, then he fell down, hitting his head on the hard cold floor.

It was hot, he could barely breath, and for some reasons it seemed as if gravity had been amplified. He raised his eyes, and he dint like what he saw, Infront of him was everyone, his whole family and friends, he even saw his mentor, his eyes were filled with fear and pity, everyone was a mess, and they were all kneeling down facing the same direction, he raised his eyes further and saw before him, Gongbao besides the new king, dressed in lavish clothes and eating the best delicacies. Gongbao turned to him with his red eyes and with a mocking tone he said, "it was all for nothing Robi, your sacrifice was for nothing," and he started to laugh, soon everyone started laughing at him, he was suffocating, the laughter seemed to be filling every pore of his being and he could feel the world around him swirling around, he was about to give up, then from a distance he heard his mentors voice urging him to keep fighting. "You don't get to quit Robi, not now, not never," and just like that, he woke up from his nightmare

"well you really do sleep like a baby dragon." The woman brought robi back to the present, he realized that he was now in a bed, dressed up and clean, a complete contrast of what he remembered of himself.

"Are you hungry?" the woman asked. Robi only stared at her, he had not fully grasped the circumstances of her actions.

" I guese that's a yes," she rose up and went and brought him the meal she was unable to eat.

The sight of food brought Robi back to life, he quickly grabbed the plate and sunk his teeth on the food, and to him it was like the best food he had ever had. For the few minitues it took him to finish the food, he din't notice anything else apart from his food. The young woman just looked at him, woundering if she had made the right decision. Robi finished his meal and asked for more, and then asked for a little more and for the first time in a few days his belly was full.

The woman took a nearby old chair and went and sat next to him and aimed directly at his eyes. " Now it's time to talk. Who the hell are you?"

"Who I am and what I want is not important, Who they are and what they want is what you should be asking." Robi said

" look here young man, I don't have time for your stupid riddles, you better start talking or I throw you out of my house." The woman was now showing signs of irritation

"The shirmas," Robi's face was now serious and full of worry

Just the mere word of the ruthless warriors was enough to send shivers down anyones spine. "What the hell is some peasant like you have to do with the shirnas?" she was now worried

"Because of this." Robi reached under his cloak and pulled out a well sealed scroll, anyone who had stayed long in the kingdom wouldn't need a second look to know that that was the scroll of the supreme, a scroll that had all the royalty lineage of the kingdom, it was highly regarded by the whole kingdom, it was their symbol of unity and it was in the custody of the king, always guarded, to loose the scroll was a kings worst nightmare, it meant that he no longer had control over the whole kingdom. And now that Robi had the scroll, it meant that unless the king got the it back, he had no control over the kingdom.

"Do you have a death wish, how did you even get your hand on something like this?" the young woman had a lot of questions.

"I don't have time to explain everything, they will be here soon and they will torch the whole village just to find me." And as if to confirm his assertions, they heard cries and commotion outside and they knew that the Shirmas were already there, and people had already began suffering for hi sins.

"Listen to me, I need you to take this scroll and keep it safe, we can't let them take it back, not after all that we've sarcrificed."Robi said this trying to convince the woman. The woman just looked at him with uncertainty, she started to wounder if she had made the right decision to allow the man inside her house. She tried to picture how this event was going to change her life, she closed her eyes, took a deep breath and made her decision.

"Wait! How are you sure they won't make sure that you have the scroll?" The woman asked

"The shirmas have been chasing me for two days now, once they get me their ego will cloud their judgement, they wont bother to look at the moment. Its their nature." Robi explained.

"Are you sure?" she asked.

"I'm positive." Robi assured her. She then took the scroll from Rob's hand, the soft texture of this ancient piece of work made her hands tremble. In her hands she held

Don't miss out!

Visit the website below and you can sign up to receive emails whenever Seth. H . Mumba publishes a new book. There's no charge and no obligation.

https://books2read.com/r/B-A-UJPTB-VAXQD

BOOKS 2 READ

Connecting independent readers to independent writers.

Also by Seth. H . Mumba

The Predator's Bait

www.ingramcontent.com/pod-product-compliance
Lightning Source LLC
Chambersburg PA
CBHW031133160726
47989CB00017B/2905